Old People, Frogs, and Albert

NANCY HOPE WILSON

Old People, Frogs, and Albert

Pictures by Marcy D. Ramsey

A Sunburst Book   Farrar Straus Giroux

Thanks to Michael Daley, Jessie Haas,
and especially Cynthia Stowe

Text copyright © 1997 by Nancy Hope Wilson
Illustrations copyright © 1997 by Marcy D. Ramsey
All rights reserved
Distributed in Canada by Douglas & McIntyre Ltd.
Printed in the United States of America
First edition, 1997
Sunburst edition, 1999
5 7 9 10 8 6 4

Library of Congress Cataloging-in-Publication Data
Wilson, Nancy Hope.
    Old people, frogs, and Albert / Nancy Hope Wilson ; pictures
by Marcy D. Ramsey. — 1st ed.
        p.   cm.
    Summary: Fourth-grader Albert is afraid of the old people at the
nursing home near his school, until he goes to visit Mr. Spear, the
elderly man who has helped him with his reading.
    ISBN 0-374-45615-1 (pbk.)
    [1. Old age—Fiction. 2. Reading—Fiction.] I. Ramsey, Marcy
Dunn, ill. II. Title.
PZ7.W6974501   1997
[Fic]—dc21   97-4986

In memory of
Raymond W. Spear
1891–1981

Old People, Frogs, and Albert

One

The only part of walking home that Albert didn't like was passing the Pine Manor Nursing Home. He liked the houses right before it. He slowed down to look at them. There were three in a row: pale green, pale gray, and pale blue. They all had white porches with fancy trim that looked a lot like lace.

A couple of girls went by, talking and laughing. They were fourth-graders, too. One of them was Tiffany, from Albert's class. They didn't seem to notice him—or anything else. They didn't even notice Pine Manor.

Albert straightened his shoulders. His backpack settled a little and seemed to get lighter.

Maybe this year he could learn not to let Pine Manor bother him. He would walk right by, the way Tiffany did.

But the long, sagging porch of Pine Manor came right out to the sidewalk.

"Hello, there," called a crackly voice.

Albert looked up. There they were: old people, slumped in their wheelchairs and rocking chairs. One woman's face folded into her mouth like a rubber mask. Another woman had hair that stuck out wild, like a costume wig.

An old man was smiling. His brown skin was as wrinkled as dry leaves. "Hello, there," he said again.

Albert's cheeks felt hot. "Hi," he mumbled, and hurried on by.

He loved the house right after Pine Manor. Last spring a fountain had been set up in the yard. It had three frog statues in the middle, and water spouted from their mouths. Frogs were Albert's favorite creatures on earth. He stepped nearer to the fountain, until a little fine spray cooled his face. But his backpack seemed heavy

again. All the way home, he felt that he was carrying a big weight.

There was a letter for him on the kitchen counter.

"Hi, honey," Mom called from her office. "You got a letter from Grammy."

Grammy was an old person, but *she* drove all over the country in a beat-up camper. She had a fancy camera and took photographs of birds.

The stamp on the letter was a picture of a red bird. Albert made sure not to tear it when he opened the envelope.

"Dear Bertie," Grammy had written. Why was her printing so wobbly? "Guess what happened . . ."

Mom came out of her office, but she hadn't turned off her computer. Albert could hear it humming. Mom wrote magazine articles and always had deadlines. "Do you want any help with that?" she asked.

Albert almost handed her the letter. Then he remembered: he could read just fine now, at least that's what the school had said. This year, he didn't need special help anymore.

"That's okay," he said to Mom. He folded Grammy's letter and slid it back into the envelope.

"But, Albert," Mom said, "don't you want to know what it says?" She held out her hand for the letter. "Come on. I'll help."

"No," Albert said, a little too loud. He put the letter in his backpack. He would read it the next day to his friend Mr. Spear. Mr. Spear was an old person, too, but he lived by himself in a house beyond the school. He still split his own stove wood for heat. Ever since Albert could remember, Mr. Spear had come into school twice a week, just to listen to kids read. And Mr. Spear had always liked Grammy's letters.

Two

In school the next morning, Albert transferred the letter to his pocket. Mr. Spear would be there at reading time.

"Who wants to read with Mr. Spear today?" Ms. Dali asked. Mr. Spear waited at the front of the room. His hair was so white it was almost yellow. It was combed very smooth, with a perfect, straight part.

Albert was sure his hand had been the first to shoot up, but Ms. Dali called on Tiffany.

Tiffany rose from her desk without hurrying. She tossed back her long hair. Tiffany had never needed special help with anything.

"Just fifteen minutes, Tiffany," Ms. Dali said. "Then, Albert, you can go."

Mr. Spear smiled at Albert. When Mr. Spear smiled, his cheeks pushed his glasses up into his eyebrows.

"I'm reading a new novel," Tiffany told him, loud enough for everyone to hear. She held up the book. "One hundred and eighty-nine pages!" Mr. Spear turned his smile toward Tiffany, and they both left for the library.

Albert watched the clock. It would take two minutes to walk down the hall, so he'd leave in thirteen. But when he got there, Tiffany would insist on finishing a whole page. Maybe he'd better leave in eleven.

After ten minutes, Albert stood up. Ms. Dali glanced away from her own reading, but didn't check the clock.

It took only one minute to get to the library. The couch at the back was reserved for Mr. Spear. Tiffany sat next to him, reading as fast as a teacher.

Mr. Spear saw Albert and smiled.

Tiffany looked at her watch. "Hey, that wasn't fifteen minutes!"

"I like an eager reader," Mr. Spear said, but he let Tiffany finish the chapter.

Tiffany was reading a great story about kids finding a magic land in an old wardrobe. Albert tried not to listen. He was glad when she finally closed the book and left.

"So, young man," said Mr. Spear, "what'll it be today?"

Albert sat down next to him. "A letter," he said. "It's from my grandmother."

"The one who calls you Bertie?"

"Yeah, so it's probably funny."

He took out Grammy's letter and smoothed it on his knee. Mr. Spear smelled like soap and the smoke from his woodstove. Albert could hear him breathing: *fwih haaaa, fwih haaaa, fwih haaaa.*

Albert started to read. Grammy's writing did look wobbly. "Dear Bertie, Guess what happened yesterday? I was riding on a . . ." Albert paused. Mr. Spear's breathing went right on, calm and steady: *fwih haaaa, fwih haaaa.* ". . . burro on an old . . . ca . . . canyon . . . I was riding on a burro

on an old canyon trail. We were going down a steep part, when suddenly the blasted cr . . . crea . . . creature stopped short, and your old grammy tumbled right over his head." Albert glanced at Mr. Spear before he read on. "My wrist broke," Grammy wrote, "but my camera didn't! Now, isn't that good luck? After all, my old bones will mend, but a camera costs good money!"

Mr. Spear's breathing got jumpy: *fwih ha ha, fwih ha ha.* That was how he laughed. Albert could hear Grammy's laugh, too—loud, like the call of a big, crowing bird.

Albert read the last part to himself. "I'm writing this left-handed, which is why it's so squiggly. How's fourth grade? I bet you're reading just fine now. I love you, Bertie. Grammy." Her signature was in cursive, with lots of loops and a very long tail.

Albert folded the letter and put it back in his pocket.

"Hey," Mr. Spear said. "You're reading right up to par now."

"Up to par?"

"Well, up to snuff. That is, just fine—like most kids your age." Not like Tiffany, Albert almost said, but Mr. Spear went on. "Pretty soon, I bet, you'll read without even noticing the words."

Albert laughed. "Yeah, right! Nobody can do that."

Mr. Spear smiled as if he knew some big secret. "Just you wait," he said.

Three

The sun was out when Albert left school, but the air was cool, even for September. Grammy would call it "crisp." Albert squinted at the sky. It was funny to think that the sun up there was the very same sun that Grammy saw when she looked up.

He was still squinting when Tiffany passed him. She was alone today. "Hi," she said, and tossed her hair.

Albert slowed down so she'd get far ahead. He watched her pass Pine Manor without even glancing at it. He waited till she passed the frog fountain, too. She didn't seem to notice that, either.

Albert held his head up and tried to walk the way Tiffany did—quickly, but not hurrying.

There was a jerky movement on the porch of Pine Manor. Albert kept his eyes straight ahead. The movement came again, with a little flash of red. Albert's eyes felt pulled to look over there.

Someone had waved. It was the old woman with the wild hair. She was wearing a bulky red sweater. She waved again. Her hand was scrawny and crooked. Maybe she'd broken her wrist once.

Albert didn't wave back. He looked away. He tried to keep his chin up. He tried to walk fast without hurrying.

Then another flash made him look sideways again. It was the frog fountain. Albert stopped and stood still. The water was catching the sun, so it looked as if the frogs were spouting light. How could Tiffany have walked right by that?

If Grammy were here, Albert thought, she'd take a picture.

Albert wrote back to Grammy the minute he got home. He made sure to write in cursive.

"Dear Grammy, I read your letter myself. No sweat. You don't even have to print, okay? I

liked what you wrote. So did Mr. Spear. He listens to me read. He's older than you, but not too old, like those people at . . ."

Albert stopped. He bit his pencil. He thought about the wild-haired woman with the crooked wrist. Her bones looked ready to poke right through her skin. Would Grammy ever get as old as that?

He erased several words, so that all he said about Mr. Spear was "He's older than you." Then, to cover up the erased part, he added, "A lot older, I think." He kept on writing. "How's your wrist? When are you coming to visit?" Albert signed the letter "Bertie," with lots of loops and a very long tail.

"P.S.," he added. "When you were reading this, did you notice the words?"

Four

Early in October, Grammy wrote back.

"Dear Bertie, Of course I noticed the words—
every single one. All in cursive, and you even
spelled 'wrist' right. I'm impressed. I'll come for
Thanksgiving—that is, if my camper holds out,
the old junk heap! It broke down on me again
last week and I'm still sitting here in K . . ., M
. . ."—Albert skipped over the name of the
place—"where your letter caught up with me. I
have to wait for a new starter motor. But guess
what? A nice family took me in, and right in
their backyard I saw a r . . . t . . ." Albert skipped
over the name of the bird. "I took a lot of great
pictures," Grammy wrote. "So isn't it lucky the

camper broke down? See you next month. I can hardly wait. Love, Grammy." She didn't say a thing about her broken wrist.

Albert took the letter to school the next day. With Mr. Spear listening, Albert would read the name of the town and the name of the bird. Then, together, they'd look up the town in an atlas and the bird in a bird book.

Just before reading time, there was a knock on the classroom door. Albert looked up from his math paper. Mr. Spear usually walked right in.

It wasn't Mr. Spear. It was the principal. She stood by the door and talked very quietly to Ms. Dali. Ms. Dali looked sad and serious. Then the principal left.

"Class," Ms. Dali said, "may I have your attention, please. I'm afraid I have some bad news."

Albert's stomach flopped. Mr. Spear.

"Mr. Spear is in the hospital," Ms. Dali said.

Albert looked out the window at the trees beyond the playground. October had turned them yellow.

"He had a stroke," Ms. Dali said.

Albert kept looking out the window, but he listened closely to Ms. Dali. She explained that sometimes something goes wrong in an old person's brain. She explained that right now Mr. Spear couldn't walk—or talk. "But we hope he'll get better soon," she said.

Albert watched the wind grab some leaves from the yellow trees. It swirled them around all crazy. Then it let go, and they floated to the ground. Now they'd dry up and die.

Albert could hear Tiffany talking. She sounded excited. "I think we should all make cards," she was saying. "We could send them to the hospital."

"That's a nice idea, Tiffany," Ms. Dali said. "You could do that during reading time. Would anyone else like to make a card for Mr. Spear?"

Albert was still looking out the window. He wanted to raise his hand, but he couldn't make his arm work.

Even so, when Ms. Dali passed out the paper, she gave a piece to Albert.

Albert drew a frog on his card. "Dear Mr.

Spear," he wrote. "Hi. It's Albert. Remember Grammy? This time, her camper broke down. She got stuck in . . ."

Albert took out Grammy's letter. He read it through. Then he finished his note. "She got stuck in Kirksville, Missouri, and saw a rufous-sided towhee. I'll read you the letter when you come back. See you soon. Your friend, Albert."

Albert closed the card, but opened it again. "P.S.," he added. "Get better fast."

Five

Mr. Spear did not get better fast.

Albert made another card the next week, and the next. October was almost over, and still Mr. Spear did not write back. Whenever Tiffany raised her hand, Albert expected her to toss her hair and show off a letter from Mr. Spear. But even Tiffany heard nothing.

At reading time one day, Albert couldn't read. Ms. Dali had handed him a book about a woman named Sarah. That was Grammy's name, and thinking about Grammy made him think about Mr. Spear. Mr. Spear was a lot older than Grammy, Albert reminded himself. He looked hard at the words on the page in front of him, but he didn't care what they said. He wondered what it meant to read without noticing the words. It sounded like magic, but Mr. Spear had said it was possible. Mr. Spear had told him he just had to wait. But how long?

Albert watched the boy across from him. His name was Safa, and he'd moved to town this year. He'd said in class that his grandparents still lived in a faraway country called Iran. Maybe Safa felt Albert watching him, because he looked up and smiled. Albert smiled, too, but glanced away. He noticed Tiffany near the front of the room. She was biting her nails as she read. Her eyes didn't seem to be moving. Did that mean she could read without noticing the words?

Albert looked out the window. Nearly all the trees were bare now. Their branches looked like bones against the sky. He closed the book, holding his place with one finger. Quietly, he left his desk and went over to Ms. Dali.

She held up her hand so he'd wait while she finished a sentence. Did *she* notice the words? "Hi, Albert," she whispered.

"May I go read in the library?"

Ms. Dali looked at him, and her eyes seemed to get deeper. "Of course, Albert," she said.

He walked down the long, silent hall and headed straight for the library couch. He sat to one side of the middle. He opened the book and pretended that Mr. Spear was there, listening. Then Albert thought he heard breathing—*fwih haaaa, fwih haaaa, fwih haaaa.*

He stopped to listen. It was only the heater coming on in the library. How was he supposed to read with all that racket?

He asked the librarian for a piece of paper and a pencil. He made another frog card for Mr. Spear. "Hi," he wrote. "When you're not here, I don't read much. And I always notice the words. How long till I don't? Your friend, Albert. P.S. Are you getting better? I hope so."

On his way home, Albert got ahead of Tiffany, who was with a friend again. He ran straight for the frog fountain. He didn't stop at the pale houses or even slow down at Pine Manor. He

didn't look up at the porch. No one called out to him. Maybe no one was there. Maybe it was too cold for old people. Albert looked ahead toward the lively frogs.

But something was wrong at the fountain. The water had been turned off. The frogs weren't lively anymore. Albert reached out to touch one, but it felt so cold that he drew his hand back.

"Dear Grammy," he wrote when he got home. "Don't get *too* old, okay?"

Six

A few weeks later, in the middle of November, Ms. Dali announced, "Good news!" She waited till everyone was paying attention. Then she said, "Mr. Spear is out of the hospital."

Albert felt something jump inside his chest. "When's he coming back? Today?"

Ms. Dali didn't hear him, because everyone was asking questions all at once. "One at a time," she said, and called on Safa.

"Can he talk now?" Safa asked.

"A little, but he isn't walking much yet. He's using a wheelchair."

Albert had put his hand up, but now he took it down. He held his breath and let other kids ask the questions.

Ms. Dali explained that Mr. Spear wouldn't be coming to school—not right away. He was much better, but he still needed lots of help and care. He couldn't live alone anymore. "At least he'll be living nearby," she said, "right up the street at the Pine Manor Nursing Home."

"Great!" Tiffany burst out. "Can we go visit?"

Albert looked out the window. He could still hear Ms. Dali's voice, but something louder was rushing in his head. Pine Manor. Mr. Spear was in Pine Manor. Albert squeezed his eyes shut. He hoped Ms. Dali would stop talking soon. He hoped kids would stop asking questions. He wanted to do a hard math paper or something. He didn't want to think about Mr. Spear in Pine Manor.

"Albert?"

Ms. Dali was looking at him as if waiting for an answer.

"What?"

"Would you like to see Mr. Spear?"

Albert's mouth felt dry. He could see Tiffany smiling from the front of the room. "Sure," he said. Of *course* he wanted to see Mr. Spear. He wanted to see Mr. Spear walk into the room right now, his hair combed slick and his glasses pushing up into his eyebrows.

"Well," Ms. Dali said. "If you both want to, I guess we could do that."

Do what? Albert wondered, but Ms. Dali went right on.

"I'll call your parents during recess," she said.

She was calling kids' parents?

Ms. Dali handed out a math paper. "This one's tricky," she said, "so pay attention."

Albert had to wait till recess to ask someone what was going on. Safa was standing alone by the school wall, hunched over against the cold wind. Albert went up to him.

"Hi," Safa said.

"Hi."

"Cold."

"Yeah."

"Too bad about Mr. Spear."

"Yeah."

"He was kind of your friend, right?"

"Yeah."

Safa was quiet for a minute. Albert took a breath, then came right out with his question. "Why's Ms. Dali calling our parents?"

"Not *our* parents," Safa said. *"Your* parents. Yours and Tiffany's. You were the only ones who said you wanted to go."

"Go where?"

Safa looked at him. "Weren't you listening?"

"Not exactly."

"You're going to visit Mr. Spear."

"But he's in . . ." Albert didn't finish.

"Yeah. That Pine Grove place, or whatever. You walk by it, right? So does Tiffany. Ms. Dali said she'd walk up there with you."

Albert looked hard at the ground. "When?"

"Right after school—today." Albert kept looking at the ground. "That's why she's calling now," Safa said. He was silent for a minute. Then he gave Albert a soft punch on the arm. "Hey, you want to get into that kickball game?"

Albert hardly heard him. "Sure," he said. "Why not?"

Seven

Inside after recess, Tiffany was acting as if she was going to a birthday party. She made another card during reading time, and decorated it with shiny paper and glitter. "If anyone else wants to make a card," she announced, "I'll take it to Mr. Spear."

Albert had decided to tell Ms. Dali he was sick. It wouldn't be a lie. Something seemed to be squeezing his stomach. He formed the words in his mind: Sorry, I have to go straight home. But even if he went straight home, he'd have to pass Pine Manor. What if Mr. Spear was sitting on the porch? What if he was looking out the window? Could Albert walk right by Mr. Spear and not even say hello? Albert's stomach got tighter and tighter, but he didn't say a thing to Ms. Dali.

By the end of school, Tiffany had collected five cards. She fanned them out in her hands. "Mr. Spear'll be so happy!"

Ms. Dali sighed. "I hope so." She pulled on her coat. "Are you ready, Albert?"

It was strange to be walking along the sidewalk with a teacher. There was room for only two side by side, so Albert hung back. Tiffany walked fast, talking and talking to Ms. Dali. Sometimes, Albert noticed, Tiffany even had a skip in her step.

As they passed the pale houses, Albert slowed down to look at the lacy porches. The sky was too cloudy. It came right down between Albert and the houses, making them all look gray.

Ms. Dali had turned to wait for him. Tiffany had turned to wait for Ms. Dali. There, just beyond them, was the sagging porch of Pine Manor.

Albert caught up to Ms. Dali.

"Are you okay, Albert?" she asked.

Albert made himself nod.

"I know this is hard," Ms. Dali said, "and you can visit another day if—"

"Hey, if you want," Tiffany said, "I can say hello to Mr. Spear for you."

No way, Albert thought, but all he said aloud was, "I'm okay." He pushed past Tiffany to the steps of Pine Manor. He lifted his foot to the first stair. Then he looked down at his other foot, but it wouldn't leave the sidewalk.

Ms. Dali and Tiffany didn't notice. They went up the steps. The porch was empty except for the abandoned rocking chairs. A pile of dead brown leaves had collected in a far corner. Albert peered at the windows of Pine Manor. All he could see were limp lace curtains and the dull, gray reflection of the sky.

Ms. Dali came back down the steps, took Albert gently by the elbow, and led him up onto the porch. The door to Pine Manor looked new—wide panes of glass in a bright metal frame—but everything beyond it was hidden by a tight white curtain.

Then Tiffany pushed the door open. Suddenly Albert was inside Pine Manor, and the door had swung closed behind him.

Eight

They were in a big front hall with a desk at one end. A man in a nurse's uniform came up to them. "You must be Mr. Spear's visitors. I told him you were coming."

"I brought him some cards," Tiffany said, fanning them out again.

"Great!" the nurse said. "He's in the day-room. Would you come this way, please?"

Albert kept his eyes on the scuffed heels of the nurse's white shoes. They went into a bright room. Without looking up, Albert could tell that there were old people sitting around. He could feel them watching him. The nurse's feet stopped.

"Mr. Spear," the nurse said cheerfully, "your visitors are here!"

The nurse stood aside, and there in front of Albert sat an old man slumped in a wheelchair. He looked at Albert and smiled, except that half of his face couldn't smile at all. Albert tried to smile back, but none of his own face would work right.

"Hello, Mr. Spear," said Ms. Dali. "Do you remember Albert? And Tiffany?"

Tiffany stepped between Albert and the drooping old man. "Hi, Mr. Spear," she said. "How are you feeling?" Her voice had gone all sweet, as if she were talking to a little kid.

Albert stepped back. He couldn't help it. He glanced sideways at the other old people. There was that woman with the wild hair. There was the man all dried up like brown leaves. The woman whose mouth folded in was looking straight back at Albert. He looked away, feeling his face go hot. Had she *winked* at him?

Ms. Dali and Tiffany were talking to Mr. Spear. At least Ms. Dali used her regular voice.

Albert tried to think of something to say. He could tell Mr. Spear about Grammy coming for Thanksgiving. He almost stepped forward to speak. Then he noticed Mr. Spear's hands. One of them lay limp in his lap. The other was trying to open Tiffany's glittery card. Tiffany took the card back and held it open for him, like a teacher showing the pictures in a picture book. Then she read it aloud.

Mr. Spear couldn't even read anymore?

Albert had to get out of there.

"Bye," he mumbled in Ms. Dali's direction. "See you tomorrow, okay?" He didn't wait to be sure she'd heard him. He turned around and hurried out of the room, through the big hall, and out the door. He left that sagging porch behind, but up ahead, instead of the frog fountain, there was a mound of cold blue plastic. The frogs had been covered for the coming winter.

Nine

When Albert got home, he was glad that Mom was in her office.

"How was your visit?" she called.

Albert didn't answer.

"Albert?"

Albert made his voice sound cheery. "Hi, Mom!"

"I'll be done here in a second, okay? There's a letter there from Grammy—and that package is for you."

Albert took the letter and the package to his room. Grammy had sent a picture of herself in a boat with swampy tree branches overhead. Her hair was all wild, but she was smiling so that her teeth showed. Albert looked at her arms. She was wearing a long-sleeved shirt. He couldn't even see her broken wrist.

Grammy wrote about looking for huge white birds called egrets. She told him about crocodiles and water snakes.

Her signature had lots of loops and a very long tail.

"P.S.," she added. "I don't look *too* old, do I? You'll see for yourself pretty soon. But remember, Bertie. No matter how old I get, I'll still be your Grammy—and still love you. Got that?"

"P.P.S. I sent you a book, but it may not get there before I do. Guess what it's about?"

"Birds," Albert answered out loud as he opened the package.

But the book wasn't about birds. On the cover was a picture of a large frog in the hands of a boy about Albert's age.

Albert opened the book and started reading. It was about a lonely kid who loved to catch frogs, but always let them go, because he loved frogs even more than catching them.

Then the boy caught a huge bullfrog, bigger than both his hands. It was special. He had to keep it. He showed it to other kids and let them hold it. Suddenly everyone seemed to like him. There was one girl, though, who kept telling him to let the frog go. She called him a jerk.

When the bullfrog in the story died, Albert looked up from the page.

Then Mom was at the door. Albert hadn't heard her come upstairs. "Ms. Dali called," she said, "and—oh, honey, you're crying!" She started toward him. "Ms. Dali *said* you might be upset."

"I'm okay," Albert said. He held out the book. "It's just sad."

Mom looked confused. "You're crying about Grammy's book? You mean you read it already?"

Albert shook his head. "I'm not quite finished." He wiped his eyes on his sleeve.

"But, Albert," Mom said, "I didn't know—I mean, how did you—"

"Don't worry," he said. He sniffed and made himself smile. "I'm fine. I just have to find out what happens." He bent his head to the book again.

Ten

At school the next day, Tiffany seemed unusually quiet. She didn't tell people about Mr. Spear. She didn't toss her hair, either. Maybe even for Tiffany the visit to Pine Manor hadn't been easy.

On the way out to recess, Safa came up beside Albert. "Did you go see Mr. Spear?"

Albert stopped and crouched down to tie his shoelace. "These never stay tied," he said.

"That's why I get Velcro ones," Safa said.

They smiled at each other as Albert stood up. "You want to play kickball again?" he asked quickly.

Their team was way ahead at the bell, and they slapped hands as they went inside. Safa didn't mention Mr. Spear again.

At reading time, Albert asked to go to the library.

"Sure," Ms. Dali said, but then she touched his arm. "Albert," she whispered. "Sorry about yesterday. It was too hard. I shouldn't have—"

"That's okay," Albert said. "Can I go now?"

Ms. Dali nodded.

In the library, Albert didn't even try to read. He sat on the couch to one side of the middle. He listened to the heater. *Fwih haaaa. Fwih haaaa.* He pretended it was Mr. Spear breathing—not the old man in Pine Manor, but the real Mr. Spear, Albert's friend.

Albert wished he'd brought Grammy's book to school. *Fwih haaaa, fwih haaaa* went the heater. He could read that story again and again. He could read it a hundred times. *Fwih ha ha, fwih ha ha.* The heater sounded like Mr. Spear laughing. Albert closed his eyes. He imagined Mr. Spear sitting next to him, smelling of soap and wood smoke. *Fwih ha ha, fwih ha ha.* What was he laughing about?

Suddenly Albert stood up. He sat down again. He tried to remember holding Grammy's book. He tried to remember feeling it in his

hands, seeing the words on the page. He *must* have seen the words in order to read them, but he hadn't noticed them. He'd noticed only the pictures in his mind—of the bullfrog, of the boy kneeling in the dirt to dig a little grave.

Fwih ha ha. Fwih ha ha.

"Hey!" Albert said, and stood up again.

"Shhh," the librarian said.

Albert wanted to yell. He wanted to run. He wanted to yell and run and laugh all at the same time.

Albert ran straight home after school. He didn't stop to look at the lacy porches or Pine Manor or the frogs covered in blue. He burst into the kitchen at home, dumped his backpack on the table, and ran upstairs.

"Hi, honey," Mom called. "Guess who's—"

"I'll be back soon," Albert said as he clomped downstairs again. He had Grammy's book and was heading outside.

"What's the hurry?" Mom asked. "Where're you going?"

"Pine Manor. Mr. Spear. Back soon. I have to run!"

Eleven

Albert made sure not to slow down until he'd run right up the steps of Pine Manor. He stopped to ring the doorbell, but there didn't seem to be one. Had Ms. Dali knocked? Albert peered at the white curtain on the inside of the glass door, but he couldn't see beyond his own reflection. He looked at the floating image of himself. His hair was sticking up funny. He smoothed it down. Would Mr. Spear be glad to see him? After yesterday, Albert wasn't sure. He thought about going home. He could write Mr. Spear a letter.

No. He folded his arms around the book and held it tight to his chest. He leaned into the door of Pine Manor and stepped inside.

There were old people sitting in the hall today. Albert glanced at them, looking for Mr. Spear. They were all strangers. A woman with only a few strands of hair reached out to Albert as if she knew him. Albert nodded to her. "Hi," he said. Did anyone come to visit her, or had people stopped caring when she'd gotten so old? Albert bowed his head and hugged his book.

"Well, hello again!"

It was the same nurse. This time, Albert noticed his name tag: Mark Thayer, R.N.

"Mr. Spear," Albert said. "Can I see him again?"

"Of course! Right this way."

Mr. Thayer gestured with his arm for Albert to go ahead of him. Albert walked toward the dayroom. He was sweating now, under his jacket. He kept his head up. He looked at the old people he passed. Someone smiled at him. Someone watched him closely with keen dark eyes. He could see Mr. Spear across the room. His hair was so white it was almost yellow, and it was combed with a perfect part.

"Mr. Spear," the nurse called. "Look who's back!"

Mr. Spear turned his head toward them. He looked blank for a second. Then one side of his glasses rose up into his eyebrows. He was smiling all crooked, but he was definitely smiling.

Albert walked right up to him. "Hi."

Mr. Thayer brought over a chair, and Albert sat down. There were other old people sitting near. Albert opened the book and began to read. His voice sounded like a whisper, but he couldn't make it louder.

Then he heard breathing. He stopped for a second, just to listen. *Fwih haaaa. Fwih haaaa.* Mr. Spear smelled of soap and medicine now, but he still sounded the same.

Albert laid the book on his knees and took off his jacket. Then he read with his full voice. He read about the boy keeping the bullfrog. He read about the bullfrog dying. He had to stop and swallow hard. There was a hush in the room, and he knew everyone had been listening. Everyone was waiting for him to go on.

Slowly, Albert read the story to the end. Without the huge bullfrog, the boy was lonely again. He was sitting on a rock by the pond when someone came up and sat near him. It was the girl who'd called him a jerk. She told him she'd killed a turtle once by keeping it too long. The two of them sat and listened together to the croaking chorus of frogs.

Albert closed the book. The room stayed quiet.

Albert leaned toward Mr. Spear. "Guess what," he said. "Even the first time I read it, I didn't notice the words."

Mr. Spear reached out and clapped his hand on Albert's shoulder. He seemed to concentrate hard for a minute. Then he said at last, "I told you so." *Fwih ha ha. Fwih ha ha.* Mr. Spear was laughing.

Twelve

"Sad story, young man," said someone with a crackly voice.

Albert looked at the man with the dry-leaves face. His wrinkled brown hand was just swiping at his cheek. "I found a blue frog once," the man said.

Albert knew he'd meant *bull*frog, but he didn't want to be impolite. He nodded, mumbled "Yeah," and tried to smile.

"No, really. A *blue* frog," the man said. "And we weren't in some rain forest. Just camping in Vermont. I couldn't believe it, either. Blue as your shirt there."

Albert looked down at his blue sweatshirt.

"So'd'ya keep it?" asked a woman with a

thick voice. Albert turned in his chair. There was that rubber-mask face with the mouth all folded in. The woman winked at Albert.

"Snakes," said another woman, the one with the wild hair. "I always liked snakes."

"That's all very well, Mrs. Wadkins," said the first woman. She held her chin high. "But the boy here was readin' 'bout frogs, and I was asking Julius a question." With one sharp nod of her head, she turned away from Mrs. Wadkins. "Now, Julius. Did you keep that blue frog or not?"

"Nah, Florence," Julius answered. "Wanted to. But my grandchildren made me let it go." He chuckled, then spoke to Albert. "They were about your age then."

"There's a bullfrog out back in that swamp," Florence said. "Hear him every spring." Without warning, she sat up tall and made a big, loud, croaky, gulping sound: *Gagagomp. Gagagomp.* It sounded exactly like a frog.

Mr. Spear started laughing, but Albert stared at Florence. "Hey, do that again," he said. "I mean, would you please?"

Florence let out four deep croaks in a row.

"Snakes are nice and quiet," said Mrs. Wadkins.

Mr. Thayer came hurrying in, holding the end of his stethoscope as if he'd been checking someone's heart. "Are you all right, Mrs. Petruski?"

"Fine," Florence said, and winked at Albert.

"I think," said Julius, "my grandson still has some snapshots of that blue frog. I'll ask him. When're you coming back, young man?"

Albert looked at Mr. Spear. "Soon," Albert said, and Mr. Spear's face seemed to smile all over.

"Good," Florence said. "I'll teach you how to croak."

When Albert left Pine Manor, he jumped down the steps with his book under his arm. He stopped at the frog fountain and listened, imagining he could hear the frogs breathing under the blue plastic. Like real frogs, they were still alive—they'd just gone deeper, out of sight.

All the way home, Albert practiced croaking like Florence.

"My goodness, Bertie! Have you got the hiccups?"

Albert looked up to see Grammy standing beside her camper in the driveway. Mom was there, too, and laughed at his surprise.

"You came early!" he said.

"I tried to tell you," Mom said, "but—"

"Well, don't stand there, Bertie. Come give me a hug!"

"A whole week early!" Albert said as Grammy squeezed him hard.

Grammy held him at arm's length. "Now take a good look," she said. "Am I getting too old?"

Grammy didn't look old at all. She just looked like Grammy. He hugged her again, and the book in his hand patted her on the back. "You can get too old if you want," he said, and Grammy laughed like a loud, crowing bird.

"Albert," Mom said, "someone called to ask you to his house. A boy named Safa? I said you'd call him back."

"Ah!" Grammy said. "You have a new friend?"

Albert nodded. Suddenly, it seemed, he had several new friends. "I love this book you sent," he said to Grammy. "Come on. I'll read it to you."